Jacob's Car Park

Story by Jill McDougall

Illustrations by Olya Badulina

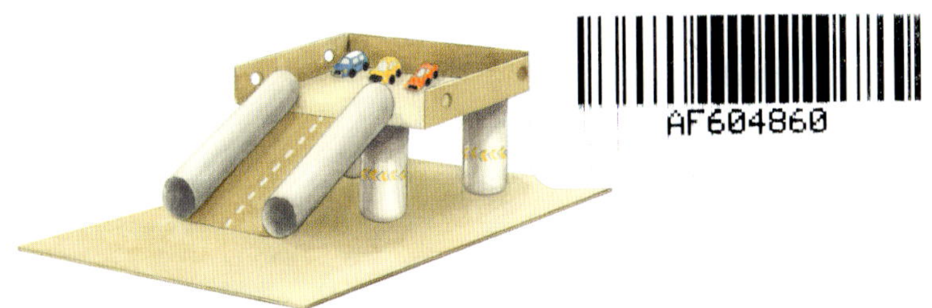

Contents

Chapter 1

Something Special for Jacob

"I'm making something special for you,"
Abby told her little brother, Jacob.
"It's a car park for your cars."

Jacob did not look at Abby.
He was carefully putting his toy cars
in a neat line.

Abby knew Jacob would get upset or angry
if his cars were not lined up.

"This car park will help to keep your cars in a line," Abby told Jacob. "I've made it out of old cardboard boxes and rolls from paper towels."

Jacob came over to the table. His eyes shone when he saw the car park.

"You can play with it tomorrow," said Abby, smiling. "First, I have to put on a ramp so the cars can get up to the top."

Chapter 2

The Car Park Is Missing!

After Jacob went to bed,
Abby made a ramp for the car park.
Then, she left the car park on the floor
next to the recycling basket.

She would show it to Jacob in the morning.

But the next day, the car park was missing!

"Dad!" cried Abby. "Have you seen a car park made from cardboard boxes and rolls? It was for Jacob's cars."

"Oh, no!" said Dad. "It looked like recycling, so I took it outside to the recycling bin. The recycling truck comes today."

Abby and Dad rushed outside.

The recycling bin was empty,
and the recycling truck was disappearing
around the corner!

"I'm so sorry!" said Dad.

"Now it's too late to save the car park.
It will be broken up in the truck."

"Jacob will be very upset," said Abby, sadly.

Jacob cried and cried when Abby told him about the car park.

"I want my car park!" he shouted. "I *need* it *back*!"

Abby knew that Jacob did not mean to shout so loudly.

Dad held Jacob close to him. "Let's go to the recycling yard," he said. "Maybe we can get some cardboard boxes and rolls to make another car park."

Chapter 3

At the Recycling Yard

There was a little shop at the recycling yard. Abby and Dad went inside with Jacob.

The shop was full of all sorts of recycling. Suddenly, Jacob shouted, "Look, look, *look*!"

Jacob's car park was on a table in the shop!

"The driver of the recycling truck saw the car park on the ground," said the woman in the shop. "It must have fallen out of your recycling bin."

"I'm glad you kept it," said Abby.

The woman smiled. "I like your car park," she said. "I even took a photo to put on our website. Other children might try making something out of recycling, too."

On the way home,
Jacob held onto the car park tightly.

Abby smiled at him.
"Next time, we can make something together,"
she said.

"Yes!" shouted Jacob. "Yes, yes, *yes*!"